make and do
★Princesses

Illustrated by
Marion Billet

STERLING CHILDREN'S BOOKS
New York

Watch the garden change on each page!

Meet Princess Pia

Princess Pia lives with her father, King Cosmos, her mother, Queen Quince, and Bella the cat.

Color in Pia and her family.

Draw over the dotted lines to write our names.

Pia

Bella

Can you spot

3 roses? 1 rainbow? 4 birds?

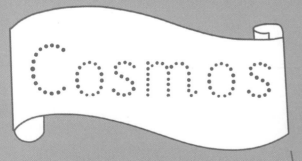

Cosmos

Quince

Pia's Palace

Pia lives in the royal palace. Use your stickers to finish the picture.

Add a flag sticker to each flagpole.

Stick fruit on the trees.

Can you stick someone or something in every window?

How to Draw Princess Pia

Follow the steps and draw Pia in the box below.

Now color in your picture!

Bella's Adventure

Follow the paw prints to find out where Bella, Max, and Chloe have been playing today.

Tall Tree Woods

The Grand Lake

The Palace Gardens

Chloe

Max

Can you count 10 yellow flowers in the grass?

Bella

Getting Ready

Use your stencils to draw the friends' outfits.
Then color them.

Don't forget our crowns!

Can you find

 A pink purse?

 2 purple shoes?

 A brown hat?

Meet Pia's Friends

Follow the lines to see which pet belongs to which friend.

Use your stickers to place our pets next to us.

Princess Bibi

Princess Molly

Prince Paulo

Mimi Mouse

Freddie Frog

Peter Puppy

10

The King's Crown

Color the sparkling jewels on
the King's crown.

Real crowns
can be very
heavy to
wear.

How many can you count on the crown?

 Stars

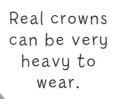 Hearts

 Circles

 Squares

 Diamonds

The Kind Frog

Pia's favorite fairytale is about a frog prince.
Help color in the pictures to finish the story.

The princess dropped her
ball in the pond.

"If I fetch it for you, will you be my
friend?" asked a frog. "I will," she said.

The princess was cross. She told
the frog she did not want him as a
friend, which made him sad.

The princess took her ball but did not want to be the frog's friend.

"You must keep your promises," said her father.

Then she was sorry she'd been unkind. She kissed the frog.

The kiss broke a magic spell and the frog turned into a prince!

Meet the Ponies

Draw over the dots to write the ponies' names on the stable doors.

Saddle Up!

Draw arrows to match the words to the picture.

Bridle

Mane

Tail

Ear

Bow

Saddle

Can you stick some bows in Misty's mane, too?

Ponies can stand and walk when they are just a few minutes old!

At the Fair

Pia and her friends are at the fair. Use your stickers and coloring pencils to finish the picture.

Put some ice cream scoops on the cones.

Add another duck to the pond.

Add 3 more carriages to the Ferris wheel.

Join the dots to see Princess Pia's prize.

Can you spot

A balloon?

A round lollipop?

A pink crown?

Colorful Stalls at the Fair

Can you spot 6 differences between the two pictures?

Can you find

1 blue balloon?

2 dolls?

3 books?

1 green kite?

How to Draw Prince Paulo

Follow the steps and draw Prince Paulo in the box below.

1

2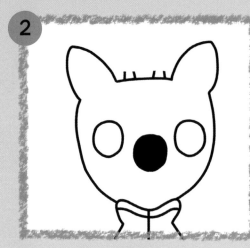

3

4

Now color in your picture!

Cute Cupcakes

Use your pens and pencils to help decorate Pia's cupcakes.

What is your favorite kind of cake?

You could add strawberries, cherries, and sprinkles.

Pia's Flower Garden

Can you find 6 differences between the two flower beds?

Can you point to something with 6 legs?

Pretty Jewelry

Can you draw some pretty jewelry inside Princess Pia's box?

Now draw patterns on my special key!

The Golden Ball

Help the kind frog find his way to the golden ball and then to Princess Pia.

How many purple fish can you count?

START

Watch out for ...

waterlilies!

fish!

Now color in Princess Pia.

FINISH

The Royal Gallery

Draw pictures of your friends in the royal picture frames.

Now color in your pictures!

Party Invitation

Help Princess Pia write an invitation to the ball.
Use your stickers to fill in the spaces.

Dear  ,

You are invited to a royal ball at

the tonight at .

Wear your best and !

I hope you can come.

Lots of love,

Princess Pia XO

Now use
your stencils
to decorate
the invitation
with hearts.

Lake Life

Princess Pia and her friends spot lots of animals at the lake. Can you finish these drawings they've started?

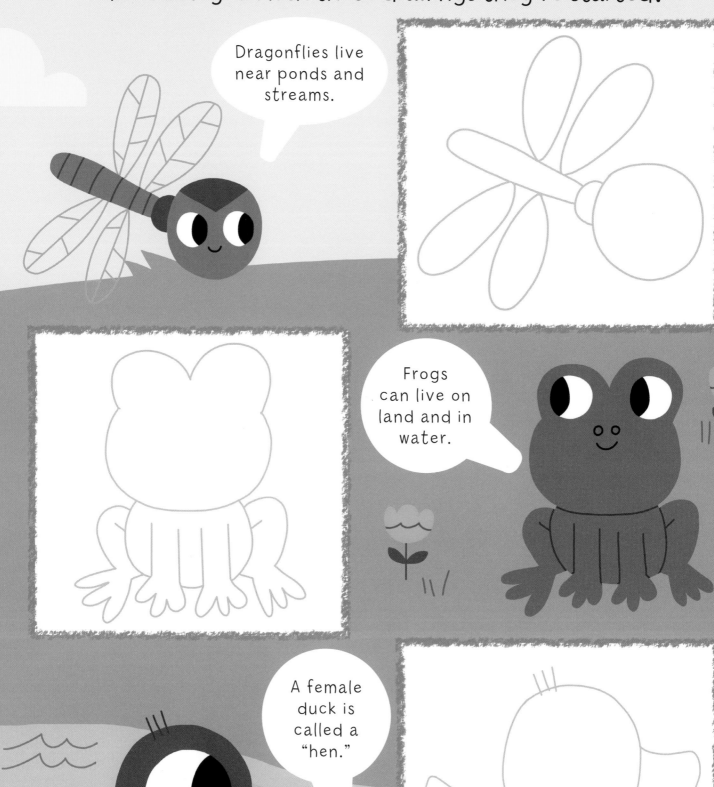

Color in the creatures with your favorite pens and pencils!

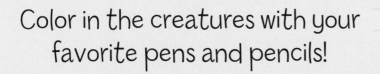

Flamingos' bright colors come from their food.

Squirrels eat mostly nuts, fruits, and seeds.

When fish swim together, the group is called a "school."

What a Performance!

Which shadow belongs to dancing Princess Pia?

1

2

3

4

5

Match the shadows

1

2

3

butterfly

cat

bird

Draw lines to match the friends to their shadows.

Matching Pairs
Pia's room is such a mess!
Draw lines to match up all the pairs.

Can you find something I might need when it rains?

Which item is the odd one out?

The Carriages Arrive

Color the carriages using the numbers at the bottom of the page.

Color by numbers

1 2
3 4
5 6

Use your stickers to put Pia's friends in their carriages.

Use your coloring pencils to decorate this carriage however you want.

Dressing Up

Pia and her friends are ready for the ball.
Use your stencils to decorate their outfits.

39

The Royal Feast

Use your stickers to give the guests their favorite foods.

Can you spot

1 star?

8 hearts?

3 drinks?

Pretty Portraits

Princess Pia is painting Princess Molly's portrait.
Help her to finish it and then color it in.

Tiara Time

Decorate the tiaras and crowns with your pens and pencils and jewel stickers.

Kings, queens, princes, and princesses wear different crowns for different royal occasions.

43

On the Dancefloor

Pia and her friends are at the ball.
Use your stencils to draw them dancing.

Even some animals and insects like to dance!

Make Princess Pia

Press out the card shapes of Princess Pia and her pretty purse. Ask a grown-up to help you follow the instructions below to make your models.

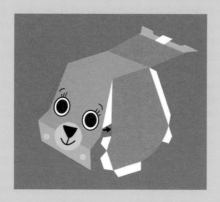

1 First make the head. Fold down the face front and sides, then take the long tab next to the eye and glue it to the inside of the head.

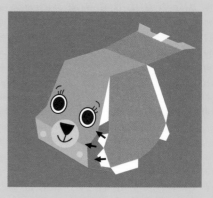

2 Bend the face to follow the line of the side section, then glue the remaining three side tabs behind the nose, mouth, and chin.

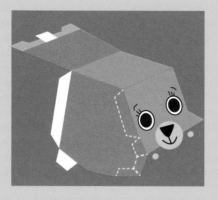

3 Repeat stages 1 and 2 on the opposite side of the head.

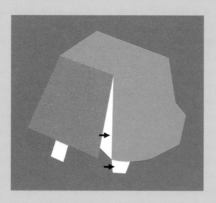

4 Fold down and glue the back of the head to each side, using the tabs on the side panels.

5 Take one ear and fold back the two small triangle tabs. Glue the tabs and stick the ear along the black dots on the top and side of the head .

6 Repeat stage 5 on the opposite side of the head.

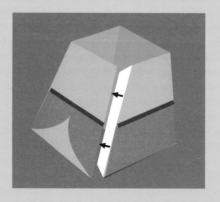

7 Fold the body into a box shape. Glue the tab along the inside edge of the model's back.

8 Take the arm section and tape a small coin to the bottom.

9 Slide the arm section into the slots on either side of the back.

10 Glue the small tab under the chin inside the center front of the model.

11 Glue the small tab on the back of the head to the inside of the body.

Purse

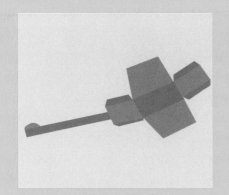

1 Now make the purse. Press out the piece and fold along the crease lines as shown.

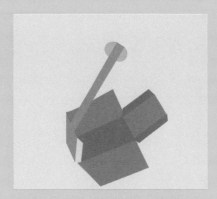

2 Stick the tabs on the end pieces inside the side pieces.

3 Fold the two round tabs on the end of the handle inward.

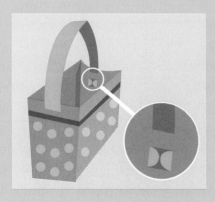

4 Find the slit at the other end of the purse and push the end of the handle through it from the outside.

5 Open out the tabs inside the purse to secure the handle.

Answers

Page 2-3 Can you spot ...?

Page 7 Bella's Adventure

Max played in Tall Tree Woods

Chloe played by the Grand Lake

Bella played in the Palace Gardens

Page 8-9 Can you find ...?

Page 10 Meet Pia's Friends

Princess Bibi and Mimi Mouse

Princess Molly and Freddie Frog

Prince Paulo and Peter Puppy

Page 11 How many ...?

Stars	★	2
Hearts	♥	1
Circles	●	5
Squares	■	7
Diamonds	◆	5

Page 15 Saddle Up!

Ear

Bridle

Mane

Bow

Tail

Saddle

Page 16-17 Can you spot ...?

Page 18-19 Can you find ...?

Page 18-19 Spot the Difference

Page 22 Spot the Difference

Page 24-25 The Golden Ball

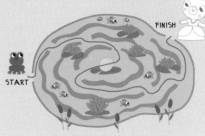

Page 30 What a Performance!

Shadow 4 belongs to Princess Pia.

Match the Shadows

1 = cat, 2 = butterfly, 3 = bird

Page 34 Lost in the Maze

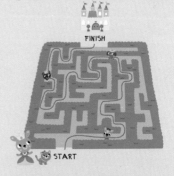

Page 35 Matching Pairs

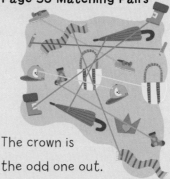

The crown is

the odd one out.

Page 40-41 Can you spot ...?

STERLING CHILDREN'S BOOKS
New York

An Imprint of Sterling Publishing
1166 Avenue of the Americas
New York, NY 10036

Originally published in 2014 in the United Kingdom by
Quarto Children's Books Ltd., The Old Brewery, 6 Blundell Street, London N7 9BH UK

ISBN 978-1-4549-1462-4
Distributed in Canada by Sterling Publishing
c/o Canadian Manda Group, 664 Annette Street, Toronto, Ontario, Canada M6S 2C8

Manufactured in China
LOT #: 2 4 6 8 10 9 7 5 3 1
12/14

For information about custom editions, special sales, premium and corporate purchases, please contact Sterling Special Sales Department at 800-805-5489 or specialsales@sterlingpublishing.com.
www.sterlingpublishing.com/kids

Illustrator: Marion Billet
Design: Duck Egg Blue
Paper Engineering: Jayne Evans
Managing Editor: Diane Pengelly
Creative Director: Jonathan Gilbert
Publisher: Zeta Jones

Stickers for pages 4–5

Stickers for page 10

Stickers for pages 14–15

Stickers for pages 16–17

Stickers for page 27

Stickers for pages 4—5

Stickers for page 10

Stickers for pages 14—15

Stickers for pages 16—17

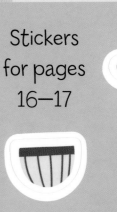

Stickers for page 27

Stickers for pages 36—37

Stickers for pages 38—39

Stickers for pages 40—41

Stickers for page 43